The Star of the New Yshan Empire

by

Michael Davies

The Star of the New Yshan Empire

For information address: info@mickiedaltonfoundation.com

First Published in 2013 in Australia

ISBN: 978-0-9875684-5-8

**Published by The Mickie Dalton Foundation
Kempsey, NSW
Australia**

www.mickiedaltonfoundation.com

Other Books by Michael Davies

The Nightmares of God
The Janus Conspiracy
Accounts of a Killing
A Friendly Killing
Dreamkill
Ready, Steady, KILL!
Mary's World
The Many Worlds of Mickie Dalton (2008)
The Many Galaxies of Mickie Dalton (2008)
The Many Universes of Mickie Dalton (2008)
*(The Mickie Dalton trilogy written with the Students of St Joseph's
Catholic High School, Albion Park)*
The Julie Malloy Gang and the Smugglers (2009)
(with the Students of Rollands Plains Upper Public School)
The Quest for the Locket (2010)
(with the Students of Comboyne Public School)
The Secret of Yuri Kirilenko (2010)
(with the Students of Byabarra Public School)
The United Nations and the Extra-Terrestrial (2011)
(with the "Bright Sparks" of Coffs Harbour Neighbourhood Centre)
The Secret of Charlotte's Cello (2011)
(with the Students of Rollands Plains Upper Primary School)
The Star of the Yshan Kings (2012)
(With the Students of Willawarrin Public School)
The War of the Yshan Empire (2013)
(With the Students of Willawarrin Public School)
The Red Fog of Time (2012)
(With the Students of South West Rocks Public School)
The Mysterious Recorder and The Door to Elsewhere (2012)
(With the Students of Gladstone Public School)
Prisoners of the Picture (2013)
(With the Students of Bellingen Public School)
And in non-fiction
The Business School Approach to Writing Your Novel

This is the third book written with the students of Willawarrin Public School to complete *"The Yshan Kings Trilogy."* Willawarrin is a tiny village about thirty kilometres from Kempsey and the school has 45 pupils. In just eight workshops, this group developed the first book in the trilogy, *"The Star of the Yshan Kings,"* a wonderfully imaginative sci-fi novel with echoes of the King Arthur legends, Arthur C. Clarke's *"2001"* and a library of Greek and Roman mythology. The second book, *"The War of the Yshan Empire"* ventured into Shakespearian Tragedy realms with echoes of *"King Lear"* and *"Hamlet,"* proving once more that not only is the imagination of children greater than we imagine, it's greater than anyone CAN imagine. This final work has echoes of Homer's Odyssey as the King returns to reclaim his Empire.

The students were:

Matilda Harris	Jacob Papalii
Jared Holmes	John Smith
Daniel O'Meara	Allan Ehsman
Jai Sammartino	Frank Smith
April Relf	Rhys Van Leeuwen
Amber Relf	Jack Saveall

Some of these students graduated to High School at the end of the second project, but we had already developed most of the story line for the final work by then, so we had a workshop by videoconference between the two schools to wrap up the project.

Sincere thanks to the Principal, Leo Hauville for his vision in initiating and supporting the continuing project. Leo retired as the project drew to a close and Murray Dickinson replaced him as Relieving Principal, continuing the support. Again, huge thanks to Simon Ferguson for his superb illustrations and to the teachers and administrative staff of Willawarrin Public school for their enthusiastic support.

Chapter 1

Commander Kyle Yshan knew he was in the battle of his life.

The alien battle cruiser was firing torpedo after torpedo at Kyle's frigate and the frigate's pilot was somehow avoiding each one with a demonstration of extraordinary flying skills.

"They're tracking us!" exclaimed the First Officer. She seemed calm, but Kyle knew she was almost certainly feeling the same high tension that he was experiencing. "Somehow they can track us while we're cloaked!"

"Navigator, how far to the wormhole?" snapped Kyle.

"Eight minutes, fifteen seconds, NOW!" replied the Lieutenant at the Nav Console.

"Guns, are the torpedoes armed?"

"Armed and ready," replied the officer at the gunnery control.

"Fire one and two," ordered Kyle. There was no sensation, but the rear screen showed two tiny sparks flying back to the invisible shape of the alien cruiser. They glowed briefly.

"Anything?" asked Kyle.

"They're still following," reported the First Officer. "They must have learned how to counteract them."

"Charlie's dad wouldn't like to hear that," said Kyle calmly, although inside he felt dismay and some fear. The torpedoes had been the critical weapon in defeating the alien fleet when it first attacked the Yshan Empire over a century ago. They had been designed by one of the most famous scientists in Yshan history, the father of Charlotte Foster, the bride of the first Kyle Yshan. Charlie was still a revered historical figure, and Kyle always revelled in the fact that she was his great, great grandmother and he had pulled many strings to get the command of this frigate, the *"Charlie Foster."*

The ship shuddered as a massive explosion occurred somewhere off the starboard side. Kyle grabbed his armrests and hung on, but several people on the bridge were knocked off their feet.

"Oooh, ever so close!" said the pilot, looking quite unconcerned.

"Report!" snapped Kyle into the ship's communications, but the only responses he got were a series of "No Damage" statements from the various locations.

"Six minutes to the wormhole," reported the Navigator. Only a slight hoarseness in his voice revealed the fear that all of them were feeling.

The frigate had been returning from a routine patrol of the borders of the old Yshan Empire, now controlled by the aliens. They had encountered the battle cruiser when they were just three light years from the old Yshan Home world but the first they knew about it was the alarm indicating an incoming missile. Only the extraordinary piloting skills of Lieutenant Bradshaw had let them dodge the missile and that was the only defence the frigate had now.

"Incoming," reported the First Officer as another missile approached.

"Got it!" snapped the pilot and calmly watched his screen as the torpedo approached, then at the last micro-second threw the frigate into a looping roll and they watched the missile flash past.

"Well done, Mr Bradshaw," said Kyle. "Nav?"

"Three minutes to wormhole."

"Sir, if they get this close, they'll be able to follow us through the wormhole," said the First Officer. Only the tightness in her hands as she clutched the arm rest of her seat betrayed the worry. "That would give away our location to the aliens."

"What a great idea, Number One," replied Kyle. "Bradshaw, can you keep us alive another three minutes."

"Yes sir!" said the pilot. "Keep watching this space!"

Kyle pressed the button on the quantum radio on his arm rest.

"Control, this is Commander Kyle Yshan. Do you read?"

The response was instantaneous. "Go ahead, Commander."

"We will enter the wormhole in two minutes. We are being pursued by a battle cruiser. It is fully cloaked but it will be just seconds behind us. Arrange a hot welcome, please. Use conventional torpedoes, the disabling systems no longer work."

"Noted, Commander," said the disembodied voice. "We're cooking up a storm for you."

Kyle grinned and disconnected the radio that used quantum physics to communicate across even intergalactic distances. Looking across at his First Officer, he saw by her own smile that she'd got the point of this manoeuvre.

For another two minutes, the deadly game continued and the pilot displayed almost magical reflexes and flying skills to avoid the torpedoes that kept coming from the invisible cruiser.

"Wormhole ahead!" reported the Navigation Officer. "Entry direction and impact speed calculated."

"Take us through, Lieutenant," ordered Kyle.

"Entering at Light998," said the Nav Officer.

The massive ring of fire that was the wormhole blazed into existence ahead and the crew barely had time to see the ring flash by. But instead of the expected sight of the stars of their home galaxy covering the entire field of vision, they found themselves in what seemed like a thick cloud of dust.

"Clever," said Kyle. "They've spread dust all over the place! The battle cruiser may be cloaked but the dust will reveal it. Pilot, turn ninety degrees to port, get us out of here!"

"Ninety to port, aye, sir!" replied Lieutenant Bradshaw and though nothing could be seen in the visual screens, the instruments showed the change of direction.

"Rear vision!" ordered Kyle. Just as he spoke, the screen cleared as they left the dust cloud that had been blown out by the Yshan fleet. They could now see the vast volume of space that was filled with dust and in the middle of it, the billowing clouds that revealed the transit of the enemy battle cruiser.

Massive explosions erupted around the cruiser as it was hit by conventional torpedoes. Its cloaking systems must have failed because the enormous sphere became visible and that gave the fleet fighters a chance to target it more accurately.

"They got the drives!" exclaimed the First Officer and a cheer rang out on the bridge as the cruiser became immobilised.

"Well done, everybody," said Kyle, at last breathing more easily. "Mr Bradshaw, where did you learn to fly like that?"

Lieutenant Bradshaw grinned cheerfully and switched on the automatic pilot, turning in his seat to face the Commander.

"Family archives, sir," he said. "I found out that the great grandfather of the first Josh Bradshaw had flown in what was called World War Two back on Earth. He flew a fighter aeroplane called a "Hurricane" and apparently he was a real ace! I've been able to find some film of that war when I took a trip back to Earth and I studied the flight techniques!"

"Just as well for us," said Kyle. "We should have you assigned to the Fleet Academy to teach the pilots."

The conversation was ended with a call from the First Officer.

"Fleet Admiral Bradshaw calling, sir!"

"Put him on," said Kyle and the large screen filled with the face of the Admiral, the Commander-in-Chief of the Yshan Fleet. Kyle knew the man was in his sixties but the face still exuded energy and a power of command that left nobody unaffected.

Kyle threw a smart salute. "Good morning, sir!"

"Well done, Commander," replied the Admiral. "And congratulations to your crew, they performed superbly. Though you took a bit of a risk."

Feeling the exhilaration of surviving a life-threatening battle and knowing how well the crew had performed, Kyle took a little more risk.

"Thank you, sir," he said. "But look what followed me home! Can we keep it?"

Around him, he heard the muffled laughter of his crew, also feeling the slightly unbalanced euphoria of surviving combat. The Admiral's lips twitched slightly.

"Will you promise to feed it properly and take it for walkies every day?"

The crew were struggling and Kyle knew they'd collapse into hysteria very soon.

"I promise, sir!" he said.

"Very good," the Admiral replied. "My office as soon as you can get here," and disconnected the call. But before the vision faded, Kyle was certain he heard the Admiral start a sustained belly laugh, but it was hidden behind the explosive hysteria of his own crew.

Chapter 2

The Fleet Admiral's office was spacious, with the commander's desk at one end and a conference table to seat twenty at the other. In between was a more casual area, a coffee table with four armchairs around it.

Kyle walked in as the door was opened by a young woman lieutenant who served as the Admiral's executive assistant. He threw a smart salute at the Admiral seated behind his desk. The older man stood up and smiled, pointing at the coffee table.

Around the walls was a series of portraits of every generation of the Bradshaw and Yshan families. Immediately behind the Admiral's desk was a set of five portraits. The first Kyle Yshan, Duke of the Moidari Sector, Guardian of the Six Home Planets and

Prince of the Royal House of Yshan looked out at the room with a faint smile of pride, as if aware of his descendents. Next to him was the painting of his wife, Charlotte Foster, once of Australia, Planet Earth, always known as Charlie. Next to Charlie, the face was of a slight, fair-haired, handsome young man, the last Yshan Emperor, Garamax 19th who had been poisoned by his cousin, Sophie, the twin sister of Kyle. Next was the first Josh Bradshaw. Like Charlie, he was originally of Australia, Planet Earth and he looked sternly out onto the room.

The final picture was of a tall, handsome woman in the uniform of the Fleet and the badges of rank of an Admiral. This was the legendary Kandria Sestucal, the first Admiral of the Imperial Fleet after it had fled to the new Galaxy. She had vanished just ten years after that event, leaving no traces of any kind or any clues as to what had happened.

These five had been the principal players in the drama that had ended with the defeat of the Yshan Empire by the alien forces that now controlled it and the flight of the remaining ships of the Yshan Imperial Fleet to a galaxy far distant from the one-time Empire. Each generation of both families had by tradition named the first-born sons and daughters with the name of the first of the line. The history of those adventures was firmly fixed in the legends of the Yshan Empire, including the story of how Emperor Garamax 19th had been found on Earth as a small boy called Henry, abandoned there by another of the Yshan line, Omaron, the Uncle of the first Kyle and his twin sister Sophie, both of them known as the greatest traitors in Yshan history. There were no portraits of either Sophie or Omaron on these walls.

Kyle was the fifth to bear the name of his ancestor. Fleet Admiral Josh Bradshaw was the fourth of his line.

"Take a seat, Kyle," the Admiral said. "Would you arrange coffee, Samalin?" he added to the assistant. Without a word, she left.

Kyle removed his uniform cap, waited for the Admiral to sit down then took a seat across from him. The placing at the coffee table indicated an informal chat, rather than a formal discussion of military affairs.

"That was quite an action, Kyle," said the Admiral.

"I'm still breathing hard," replied Kyle. "But when my First Officer said they were close enough to follow us through the wormhole, I got the idea that capturing the ship would be a good idea."

"But did you think they might broadcast the details back to their headquarters and we might expect an invasion fleet at any time?"

Kyle sat still. He realised that he hadn't thought about that and felt chilled at the idea.

"No, sir," he said softly. "That was a mistake."

"But as it turned out, a risk worth taking," the Admiral said. "Our technicians have gone through the ship's computer records and it looks like they didn't pass the details of the wormhole entry back home, only the fact that they were in pursuit of an Yshan warship. As far as the aliens are concerned, their ship has just vanished. And the main development, a massive one, is that we know now that our disabling torpedoes no longer work on their ships. Can you imagine if we'd begun the invasion of our old territories armed with those torpedoes?"

"It would have been fatal for us," said Kyle. "But now we have an alien ship to examine and find something that can damage them."

"Exactly," said the Admiral and paused as the door opened and the young woman arrived, wheeling a trolley with a coffee pot and cups and all the trimmings. She poured two cups for the men at the table and left without a word.

Kyle drank his coffee black, but he waited while the Admiral added sweetener and cream to his.

"What will you do with the crew of that ship, sir?" Kyle asked.

An expression of distaste crossed the older man's face.

"I've no idea, to be honest," he replied. "The interrogators are tackling them of course, but I doubt there's anything else they can tell us that we don't already know. I'm afraid they're facing a long period of captivity. I can't say I have any sympathy for them."

Kyle sipped his coffee and changed the subject. "Your grandson did a magnificent job avoiding the torpedoes," he said. "Apparently he's been studying fighter techniques from an old Earth war."

The Admiral smiled proudly. "So he told me! It looks like we could adopt some of those ideas for all our pilots. I've told the Academy to set up an advanced flying section to teach them. Young Josh can go and be the first instructor."

"Sir, you mentioned the invasion. Is that really in planning now?"

The Admiral looked serious. "It's been in planning ever since we came here a hundred and twenty years ago. But our first priorities of course were to set up our own nation, develop industries, towns and explore the galaxy that we'd taken over. Now we have an empire of our own, with over sixty planets colonised and prosperous and I suppose we wouldn't be too serious about returning home under normal circumstances. But the spies we've had back there report that things are ugly, just as you have also reported. Whole worlds have been looted to serve the aliens, it's a real tyranny in charge and the people are desperate. Apparently the original Sophie became Empress and she's got some descendant, also called Sophie who's just as appalling as the first. Of course, you're related to her, Kyle, so you won't like to hear that."

Kyle stirred uncomfortably. "No, I really don't," he said. "It's always worried me that the Yshan family could produce somebody as evil as Sophie and her Uncle Omaron, while the rest of us seemed to be pretty good people. It's odd that she seems to have carried on the same tradition of naming her female descendents after herself. Do we know any more about the family?"

"Not a thing," replied old Josh Bradshaw. "It's peculiar, our spies should have found out something. We've got copies of their school books and encyclopaedias but there's no mention of the first Sophie ever having a family. But the present one is clearly running a terrible regime and our people are suffering as you saw yourself. An invasion is essential."

"But they have their Star," replied Josh. "Can we invade while they still have that?"

"It's the main question," agreed the Admiral. He looked down at the medallion hanging on his chest. It was a plain silver disk but in the centre was a tiny speck of light, too small for the particle emitting it to be measured. "You and I and my sister are the only people in the Galaxy to have these. We all pray that they indicate that some day, the Star of the Yshan Kings will be reborn and guide us as it once did. The fact that these specks stay alive gives us hope that it will happen."

Kyle touched the twin of the disk hanging round

his own neck. There were only three of these, all that was left of the large crystal that had guided the Yshan family over five thousand years from a small, dying clan on a dying planet to the leadership of a Galactic Empire extending over several thousand worlds. Since fleeing the old empire, Yshan legends had grown that one day, a new star would be born, to replace the one that had died as the alien fleet had defeated the old Empire. The medallions were passed down through the generations and Kyle had received his when his father had died just two years ago.

"However," the Admiral broke into the small silence. "It's clear that the aliens don't know where we are and thanks to you, we know that the weapon we would have depended on would not work. We have the alien ship and our people are tearing it apart to work out a new weapon. So yes, Kyle, we are planning an invasion, perhaps in two or three years."

That reminded Kyle that he'd forgotten one more surprise for the Admiral.

"With your permission, Sir?" he asked as he touched the communicator on his lapel.

The Admiral nodded, with a slightly puzzled expression.

"Bring him in," said Kyle and immediately, there was a knock on the door and it opened. Two large, armed men of the Fleet Military Police walked in with a much smaller man between them. They saluted the Admiral and left.

The newcomer was small, slightly built, looked about forty years old and badly frightened.

The Admiral stared at him, frowning.

"Kyle?" he said.

"With your permission, Sir," said Kyle. "May I present a man who calls himself Omaron Yshan."

The Admiral looked shaken. "You'd better explain," he said.

Chapter 3 – A Week Earlier

Kyle and his First Officer, Martina Corralon walked slowly along the sidewalk in the city that was still the capital of the Empire. Sometimes it amused Kyle that so many women had adopted the fashion of using Earth names, ever since his great, great grandmother, Charlotte, known as Charlie had been such a famous woman.

Once, this city had been the capital of the Yshan Empire, but over a century ago, the Aliens had invaded for the second time, destroying the small number of Yshan warships that had been near the Home Planet. The remainder of the fleet had fled, able to find a new Galaxy as a result of technology developed from alien ships captured during the first invasion and adapted by the genius of the first Josh Bradshaw.

The city had little resemblance to the city Kyle knew from his history books. Then, it had been rich, sophisticated and colourful, populated by a wealthy, peaceful civilisation that had grown up through a thousand years of the Galactic Empire, governed by the Yshan Family under the guidance of the Star of the Yshan Kings.

Now the place was dull, run-down, roads hadn't been maintained in decades, buildings were similarly decrepit and the people all looked miserable and poverty-stricken. It was a depressing sight. Kyle and his officer were dressed as locals in poorly-made clothing and they fitted in with the scene to give no cause for second looks.

The only traffic on the roads was military. Several times, open trucks had drifted through, floating a metre above the ground on anti-gravity engines that let them ignore the poor road surfaces, with half a dozen armed guards sitting with weapons ready for use. All the ones Kyle had seen so far were alien, very tall, elongated beings but mostly like humans other than their height and thin build. But one of the trucks was manned by Yshans, also in uniform and carrying weapons.

"Traitors," muttered a man next to Kyle and then looked terrified as Kyle turned to him.

"Relax, I'm with you," said Kyle. "So some people have joined the occupation army?"

"Where have you been all your life?" asked the man. "Lots of them have gone over to the Empress, may she die soon."

"It's our first time here," said Martina. "My brother and I have come up to see our mother, we live a long way south. Down there, we haven't seen any police but the aliens."

"Can we talk?" asked Kyle.

The man nodded and gestured for them to follow him. He led them down an alleyway between two ruined buildings and into what might once have been a pleasant square. Now it was filled with sad-looking people, cooking various meals over open fires. Even the children looked depressed and quiet.

The man led them to one section where a woman was boiling water over a fire made of household debris.

"My wife," he said. "Can we offer you tea?"

Realising how poor these people were, Kyle and Martina shook their heads but sat down on the ground.

"This is dreadful," said Kyle. "Is it the same everywhere?"

"As far as we know," replied the other woman. "The Demon Empress Sophie rules like a tyrant. She owns all the wealth and any disobedience is punishable by death. Most of the industry is dead except for mining and the aliens take all that back to their home world."

"Sophie?" asked Martina. "It can't be the original one, she'd be about a hundred and fifty years old."

"Dunno about that," muttered the man. "We don't get any schooling, so we only know a bit about history from stories passed down by a few people. But it can't be her, this one looks about twenty, very dark, very beautiful, very evil."

"So what do you know about our history?" asked Kyle.

"Not a lot. We know that aliens came one day and the Yshan Space Fleet vanished. The legend is that the Fleet went to another Galaxy and is building itself up again. All of us grow up dreaming of the day when the Fleet returns and destroys the Aliens, takes the Empress prisoner for trial and the Old Yshan Empire will be restored."

"It's a good dream," said Kyle. "Keep a firm grip on it for it will happen some day." He stood up, followed by Martina. "We must go," he said.

They walked back along the alley to the main street and as they emerged, another man stood before them. He looked about thirty, a few years younger than Kyle but Kyle felt there was something familiar about him.

"I must talk to you," said the man. "I saw you go in there and I recognised you."

"You recognised us?" demanded Kyle. "How can that be, we've never met?"

"No, we haven't," agreed the man. "But I know who you are."

Kyle felt a twinge of worry. The man seemed desperate but there was a ring of truth in his voice. "So who are we?" he asked.

"I don't know the woman," the man muttered. "But you, you must be one of the royal family of Yshan."

Shock ran through Kyle. *How had he been recognised?*

"How do you know that?" he demanded.

"Because you look like me."

"What?" exclaimed Kyle.

"He's right," broke in Martina. "You do look similar."

"You've got to take me away from here," the man said, fear in his face.

"Why? Who are you?" asked Kyle.

"My name is Omaron Yshan," the frightened man replied.

"What?" snapped Martina. "A descendent of the original Omaron Yshan?"

"No. I am Omaron Yshan."

"You'd better come with us," said Kyle.

Chapter 4

The Admiral stared at the man standing before him.

"You say that you are Omaron Yshan, the uncle of the Princess Sophie with whom you betrayed the Empire?"

The terrified man nodded his head.

"Don't be ridiculous!" snapped the Admiral, rising to his feet. "That man must be about a hundred and fifty years old! You look about forty."

"I am Omaron Yshan," the other repeated.

"Kyle, does anyone else know about this?"

"Only my First Officer, Sir and she's not saying anything. The rest of the crew only know I brought a refugee back with us."

The Admiral turned back to the man standing alone.

"So why have you fled? I gather that you and the current Empress rule the old Empire. You must have wealth beyond imagining and power to match."

"The *current* Empress?" Omaron said with a cold smile. "This is the same Sophie. There have been no others. And she's quite mad. Somehow she got the idea that I was in contact with her twin brother and was conspiring against her for a return of the Yshan Royal Family. Once she'd decided that, my life was worthless."

The Admiral seemed to think for a quiet moment.

"Let's imagine for just a minute that this insane story is true," he said. "How do you explain your age?"

"The Star," said the man. "The Dark Star. This is one of the rewards I get for serving it."

"The Dark Star?" Kyle jumped to his feet. "It's a Dark Star? We knew you had a Star, but not one that was different from our original. And it supports you and Sophie the way the Star of the Yshan Kings guided us?"

The man nodded again.

"Where did that come from?" demanded the Admiral.

"The Aliens took me to see it when they first got me to help them."

The shocked silence in the room lasted for over a minute. Then Kyle's immobility was shattered.

"Sir, your medallion!" he exclaimed.

The Admiral stared down and then back at Kyle.

"And yours," he said.

The tiny spark on both medallions had turned into a deeper, larger and brighter glow.

"We need to have a meeting of the families," said the Admiral.

*   *   *

The two Great Families of the new Yshan System met infrequently, only when major events or dangers occurred. In the last ten years, such meetings had been only once a year and then had been mainly administrative as few dangers had threatened the system of sixty prosperous planets, all self-governed and looking to the central planet known for barely-understood reasons as "Henry," only as a figurehead for the Commonwealth of Planets.

Traditionally, chairmanship of the meetings alternated between the senior members of each family. As the technical leader of the Yshans, Kyle was entitled to take the chair this time. However, given the critical subject of this meeting, he had asked Fleet Admiral Bradshaw to run the meeting.

Kyle looked around the table. He knew all the people there, but not all were close acquaintances. Many, but not all were also Fleet Officers, a common career path for people in what were in practice, the two Royal Families of the people. Josh Bradshaw 5th, the son of the Admiral and father of the young pilot who had flown the frigate to safety was an academic, a highly regarded historian at the city's University but not a man with the charisma and energy that both his father and his son displayed.

Sitting next to the middle Bradshaw was another one in the line, the professor's daughter and elder sister of the pilot, another Charlotte, as was the tradition of the first-born daughter of the Bradshaw line who was also given a middle name of Foster. She looked nothing like her namesake as she was not a descendant of the first Charlotte Foster but Kyle found her immensely attractive and occasionally had day-dreams of another Charlotte-Kyle Yshan wedding.

"Good morning, everybody," the Admiral said with a smile and received a polite chorus from the eighteen people round the table in his office.

"Three days ago," continued the Admiral, "Commander Kyle Yshan returned from a spying mission to the heart of the enemy system, our old Home Planet. He returned with the same observations that similar missions have provided, stories of poverty, deprivation and tyranny under the alien occupiers with another Princess Sophie apparently in nominal charge as Empress. We have assumed that she is a descendent of the Sophie who allied with aliens in the act of treason that destroyed the first Yshan Empire, although we can't find any records that suggest a family line from that Sophie."

He looked around the table, making eye contact with each of the persons sitting there. He clearly had their deep attention.

"As you know, the Commander was able to persuade an alien cruiser to come back with him..." He paused as the wave of laughter ran round the group. "And that has undoubtedly saved us from disaster, as we learnt that our old disrupter torpedoes no longer work as they did in the first Battle of Home

Planet when those missiles cancelled all engine and weapons systems in the alien ships."

He paused again and saw that he still had the absolute attention of everybody in the room.

"But the Commander brought back something else," he continued. "This man."

A holographic image of the prisoner appeared in the middle of the table. Everybody's attention switched to the image.

"He claims to be Omaron Yshan," said the Admiral and stopped as a wave of shock and derision ran through the group.

"But let me stress," he continued. "Not a descendent of the original traitor, Omaron Yshan, Uncle of Princess Sophie and Prince Kyle, but *THE* Omaron Yshan himself."

The sounds around the group reflected a mixture of astonishment, disgust and mostly disbelief.

"Josh, that's got to be rubbish!" exclaimed Charlie Bradshaw, the Admiral's sister. "That original Omaron has got to be over a hundred and fifty years old! This one looks about thirty, maybe forty. Now I know that the Yshans live longer than the human line, but not *that* much longer!"

"Exactly what we thought," agreed the Admiral. "So we did some searching in the archives and we found the recording of the trial for treason of Omaron. Here it is."

The image of the prisoner was moved to the side of the room and a new image appeared. It was a scene of the trial conducted some hundred and twenty years ago, just weeks before the alien invasion of the Empire. It showed Omaron Yshan, still a prince of the Royal Yshan family, standing in the dock before the tribunal of senior Fleet officers.

A murmur of interest ran around the table. "Look at the group in the background," said the young Lieutenant Josh Bradshaw. "That's the first Josh, the first Kyle, and..."

"Good Heavens!" exclaimed the elder Charlie. "That's my namesake, Charlie Foster!"

"And mine, too, Auntie!" added the younger Charlotte."

"And that's Emperor Garamax 19th," said Kyle, pointing to the slender, fair-haired young man. "So who is the other woman? She's in Fleet uniform but I can't see the rank."

"That's my predecessor," said Admiral Bradshaw

softly. "That's Captain Kandria Sestucal before she took the others to Earth at the Emperor's orders just before the alien invasion and saved all their lives."

"This is quite fascinating, but we've forgotten the main point of showing this scene," said Kyle. "Look at the man in the dock. Is that the same man as we brought back here?"

For a few moments, everybody stared at the two images and the shock in the room was profound.

"It's the same man," said Charlie. "That's Omaron Yshan, still about forty years old."

"But Charlie, there's a problem," said Kyle. These meetings were informal. "That's certainly the man I brought back but he looks some years older than when we met him last week. I thought he looked younger than me at that point."

A murmur of interest ran round the table.

"Could that be just because of the fear and worry he's experiencing?" asked the elder Charlie.

"I'm sure that's a factor," replied Kyle. "But if he's telling us the truth and something has kept him young, then the possibility exists that the young, beautiful and evil Empress Sophie of today is the same woman who betrayed the Empire a hundred and twenty years ago."

Into that frozen scene of horror, dismay and shock, something happened that blew everything else into far less importance.

The images vanished. Instead, standing just a metre or two from the conference table a tall young woman appeared. She looked about forty, smartly dressed in Fleet uniform but without badges of rank. She smiled at the expressions around the table.

"Good morning," she said. "My name is Kandria Sestucal. I think you just recognised me in that historical scene."

The profound silence in the room lasted for over a minute. Everybody around the table knew the name of this tall young woman. It was engraved in their history and all the legends of how they found on Earth, the Prince Garamax as a young child who knew nothing of his nature and destiny. It was this woman who had led the single battle cruiser against the combined fleet of the Alien Invader and defeated them with the help of the first Josh Bradshaw, Kyle Yshan and the father of the first Charlie Foster. Later still, she was the first Admiral of the New Yshan Fleet after the flight from the Old Empire.

"Admiral Sestucal, I believe?" said the senior Josh Bradshaw, rising to his feet.

The woman smiled at him and waved him to sit down again.

"No longer an Admiral," she said. "That's your role."

"But you are that person?" insisted the Admiral, remaining on his feet. His voice was calm and controlled but Kyle thought he detected a trace of tension in the old man.

"I am," said the woman.

"In that case, you would have to be about a hundred and fifty years old," continued the Admiral. "And you still look like the pictures show you from over a century ago. So you are not Yshan. And you cannot be Human. What *are* you, Kandria Sestucal?"

She smiled again. "I think you already know, Admiral," she replied.

"You are one of the First," said Kyle, at last finding his own voice.

She turned to him, her smile even wider.

"It's so good to see you, Kyle," she said. "You look so like your ancestor, you could be his twin. And of course, you are quite correct. I am one of the First."

The Admiral sat down as if his legs had failed him.

"Why?" he demanded.

"The Yshan people need us again," the woman said. "And we need the Yshan people. We are all in great danger."

Chapter 5

Slowly, the room returned to a normal state but the after-effects of the shock remained as if a stun-grenade had gone off some moments before.

"You'd better explain," said the Admiral.

Kandria Sestucal walked to the head of the table.

"You all know your history," she began. "You know how the Yshan people were dying, starving on a world that itself was dying over five thousand years ago. We appeared then and gave the Star to the first Garamax Yshan. But you need to know, it was not just our wish to save a dying people. That planet had been our home for many hundreds of thousands of years before that, but my people had begun preparations for growing to a new stage of existence in a new, higher dimension. We needed to leave the world to somebody who would take care of it, because we still depend on the health of our planet of origin for our survival. I will explain this more at another time. But now you must understand that the world is again dying under the tyranny of Empress Sophie and her allies, the aliens who drove out the Yshan people."

She looked around the table. Every face was fixed on her.

"We must go to war again," she said. "But first, I must take the descendants of those who started this adventure so many years ago and we must go back to where it all began. There is something there I must show you and that we need. It will be vital for our battle to reclaim the Yshan Empire."

Again, she looked around the table. She moved just a little to the elderly Charlotte, the sister of the Fleet Admiral.

"Charlie, will you give me your medallion?" she asked.

Without hesitation, Charlie lifted the medallion from around her neck and handed it over. Like those around the necks of Fleet Admiral Bradshaw and the young Kyle Yshan, it was glowing with a bright, beautiful light, unlike the almost invisible gleam that all three medallions had shown for the last century or more.

"And yours, Admiral," continued Kandria and

again received the medallion without hesitation. She walked around to the youngest Josh Bradshaw and handed one to him. Astounded, he slipped the chain over his head and stared down at the silver disk.

"You also look so like your ancestor, Josh," Sestucal said softly. "And now you, Charlie," she continued and advanced on the younger Charlotte. "Time for you to take your place in history," she said and handed the medallion to the young woman who slowly put it around her neck, staring entranced at the glowing particle.

"We four must go back to where it all began," said Sestucal. "It is right that the youngest of the two families be part of this. What we do back on Earth will let us take back the old Empire."

Chapter 6

"Earth!" exclaimed Charlie. "I never knew it was so beautiful!"

They looked down at the blue, cloud-flecked planet slowly rotating beneath them.

"Nor me," said Josh, not failing to keep some tears running down his cheeks. "It's where we came from, it's the planet of our family's birth! This is my second visit and it still affects me like this."

"Where's Australia?" asked Kyle, also quite affected by the beauty of the planet Earth.

Josh pointed at the southern continent just appearing out of the night shadow on the left and emerging into clear sunlight over the whole country.

"Kandria, can you put us down in the right place?" asked Kyle.

Since leaving the home world, the three of them had slowly become accustomed to dealing with the one-time Fleet Admiral as a friend, but the awe they felt in the presence of one of the legendary "First" remained.

"Of course," she replied and her fingers ran over the computer panels as if testing the texture of a fine silk. "We're fully cloaked, so no Earth radar systems or telescopes will see us."

The three young people watched as the globe seemed to zoom closer and become a vast plain with the deep blue of the sea down the East coast and that vanished as the ship landed in a clearing in the middle of dense woodland.

"Welcome to Earth!" said Kandria as the door opened on one side.

All of them moved to the opening and stood, staring. They had all visited other planets in the Yshan Confederation and Kyle and Josh had visited their old Yshan Capital as spies, so there was no great shock in standing on a new planet under a different sun, but Earth was different. It was the home planet of Charlie's family and the Bradshaws, part of the legends taught to all schoolchildren and it was also the planet where the last Emperor, Garamax 19th had been found as a small child, quite unaware of his true nature and destiny. Only Josh had been here before, visiting to research the Bradshaw family history.

"What is that incredible noise?" exclaimed Charlie as a loud, whooping cackle began somewhere in the woods and was answered by several others around the forest.

"It's called a Kookaburra!" replied Kandria with a smile. "One of Australia's greatest symbols."

"What is it?" asked Charlie, looking nervous. "Is it an animal big enough to eat us?"

Kandria laughed. "It's a bird, Charlie! And one of my favourites! Come on, let's take a walk."

At last, they descended onto the green surface of the woods.

"This is lovely!" said Charlie. "The air is so fresh. I think I like it here!"

"Your ancestors had a property very near here. Yours too, Josh," said Kandria. "And as children, Josh, Henry and Charlie went to school, just about five kilometres away. We'll go and visit soon but there's something here you have to see."

Without any movement being seen, several people appeared in the clearing. All three of the young people let out a gasp.

"Nothing to worry about," said Kandria. "These are my people. These are the First."

* * * *

Charlie was the first to recover some sort of control. But even then, her voice was raspy with shock and she held her hands before her mouth almost in prayer.

"You are the First? The people that gave us the Star and saved the Yshan race from extinction?"

A tall, dark-haired, distinguished-looking man nearest to her replied.

"We are. It was my grandfather who gave the first Yshan the Star over five thousand years ago."

"Your... your *grandfather?*" said Josh, his voice almost a croak. "I think this is more than I can handle. How old *are* you?"

The man smiled. "I'm just a kid," he said. "Just over a thousand years."

Kandria broke into the conversation, seeing the shock in the eyes of all three of the visitors.

"Let's talk about it over breakfast," she said. "Come, I'd like to show you where we live."

She led the way into the denser wooded area and to a small hut. She opened the door to reveal a staircase.

"The hut is cloaked normally," she said. "Nobody can ever see it and even if they approached too close, we have a mechanism that will make them walk away without realising why. Our ship is protected the same way."

She began walking down the staircase, followed by everybody else.

Josh was feeling real concerns now. This did not feel like the residence of a group of people with the powers that the First had demonstrated.

But as he reached lower down the steps, the view changed his mind.

He was looking out at a beautiful and vast room, much like a ballroom of some luxurious Palace. It seemed to stretch in all directions and although he could see no light sources, the entire place was lit with a soft white glow that seemed quite even throughout.

"Wow!" he gasped and saw the same reaction in his two companions. They continued to the floor and looked around them as the others gradually came down the steps.

Although the room was underground, it seemed to be lined with windows that looked out onto glorious scenes of mountains and lakes. The ceilings were high, covered in beautiful paintings.

"This is where we live," said Kandria, breaking into the silent wonderment.

Josh looked back at the people who had followed them down, including the one man who had spoken to them so far. There seemed to be about thirty or so.

"Where are the rest of you?" Charlie asked, also looking back at the group.

"This is it," said Kandria. "This is all of us who are still left in a physical state."

Charlie took a deep breath.

"You said something like that back at the family meeting. What does it mean?"

Kandria nodded with understanding.

"We'll explain everything to you soon. But now we're going to have a nicely extended and very social breakfast and then later we'll tell you the whole story of why we saved the Yshan people so long ago and why we must do the same again. But let's get breakfast organised and then I want you to meet somebody."

Charlie smiled, seeing the warmth in Kandria and how it was affecting all her friends.

"Yes, we should have something to eat," she said with a small laugh. "After all, we've travelled over two hundred light years since our last meal!"

The other two joined in her relaxed mood and they began moving to a long dining table set at one side of the room. The tantalising smell of coffee drifted to their noses.

"But who's this little boy?" exclaimed Josh, as a small child appeared from a doorway. "He's the first youngster we've seen here."

The child stopped and stared at the three visitors with a solemn, wide-eyed look. Josh estimated he was about seven years old, almost skinny in his build, with fair hair. The boy went to Kandria and she placed a gentle hand on his shoulder.

"This is really whom you have come to meet," she said. "Your ancestors, the first Kyle, Josh and Charlie met him very close to here and they knew him as Henry. Let me present to you the Emperor Garamax 19th, seventy-second Emperor of the Yshan Galactic Empire."

Chapter 7

Breakfast was indeed leisurely, friendly and delicious. Food of every conceivable style was laid out in large bowls on the table and people took what they wanted, as and when they wanted. Tea and coffee seemed never-ending.

Josh was delighted to see his favourite dish of light, thin pancakes served with lemon and sugar, Charlie experimented and found some Asian dishes with an aroma of saffron and Kyle settled for a traditional Australian feast of bacon and eggs and hash brown potatoes.

"And now for some explanations," said Kandria as the meal ended. "Let's go to another room. Henry, will you come with us?"

The small boy followed them without a sound. He had not uttered a word since his appearance and had tucked into his own meal of toast and jam and milk, looking quite calm and self-possessed in the room full of adults.

Kandria led them into a lounge room. Armchairs were placed around the room on a deep red carpet, small coffee tables sat by each chair and the room was pleasantly warm. Drapes of various colours lined the walls. Josh thought this was quite luxurious.

"Take seats," suggested Kandria and took one herself while the others sat in places so that they could look at each other. Little Henry sat cross-legged at Kandria's feet and looked calmly at each of them. Josh felt almost un-nerved at the intense gaze, feeling the boy was reading his very soul. He smiled at him and was pleased to get a small smile in return.

"It really is Garamax," broke in Kandria.

"But how?" demanded Charlie. "The Emperor was murdered well over a century ago, poisoned by Sophie just before he left for the trip here with you and our ancestors."

"Good heavens!" exclaimed Kyle. "I've just realised! We're the same people, just later generations of that original group! Except for you, of course, Kandria! You were one of the group that actually came here with the first Kyle, Josh and Charlie."

"And Henry!" added Josh, unable to stop grinning at the same realisation.

"Yes, Henry," said Charlie. "How on *EARTH* can this be the original Henry?"

"Have you ever seen a recording of his coronation?" asked Kandria.

"I'm pretty sure we all have," answered Kyle.

"Then do you remember this bit?" continued Kandria.

The room darkened a little and in the middle appeared a holographic image of the stage of the coronation so long ago.

Henry was fifteen years old. His uncle, Karocarl, Kyle's father had been filling the position as Regent Emperor while the search for the boy continued and Henry had been found on Earth. Sitting at the rear of the stage were fifteen-year old Kyle, his mother, Josh, Charlie who was about twelve years old and Charlie's mother and father.

The Emperor Karocarl went to the stand on which was placed the Star of the Yshan Kings, the sentient crystal that had guided the Yshan Royal Family for five thousand years. The Emperor picked it up and handed it to Henry. The boy raised the crystal above his head and it immediately glowed with the light of the entire Galaxy, the sure sign that Henry was the rightful Emperor.

"But this is the critical part," broke in Kandria. "This is the second part of the coronation that has never been understood. Watch."

On the stage, the now ex-Emperor replaced the Star on its stand. He bent down behind it and brought out a circular tray that looked like black basalt. On it was a golden mask. To Josh, it looked like something he had seen in his studies of Earth, the mask of an ancient Egyptian Pharaoh, perfect in its pure lines.

"The final sign," murmured Kandria. "The rightful heir must put on the mask and it will take on the features if he's the right one. We've never known until recently where that Mask came from or how it does what it does."

Henry held up the mask for all to see then carefully slipped it against his face. Almost immediately, the metal seemed to flow like mercury, taking on the shape of Henry's face until it looked just like a golden replica of the new Emperor.

Charlie let out a small sigh. "That's the part that still blows me away! I can never get used to it and I've never understood it."

"We discovered only after we came here that it was something the Star created," said Kandria. "It was a form of insurance against exactly the events that did occur, Sophie's murder of the rightful Emperor. What the mask was doing there was literally taking a complete copy of Henry, his mind, his DNA, everything."

Josh suddenly gasped as he realised what she was saying. "So this is a clone of the original Henry?" he exclaimed.

"More than a clone," replied Kandria. "No, this IS Henry. He has been rebuilt from the blueprint the mask was holding."

"But he's only a little boy!" said Kyle. "Henry was about twenty six when he was murdered."

"And this child is a new-born infant," replied Kandria. "He appeared just a year ago as a brand new baby and that's what alerted us to the fact that the time for retaking the Yshan Empire is coming. The mask is gradually growing him back to that stage. Even after the coronation, it stayed linked to Henry's mind and stored all his memories right up to his death. In another few weeks, this little boy will be the fully grown Emperor Garamax 19th with all his memories and all the training and experiences he had before."

Josh, Charlie and Kyle stared at little Henry who looked calmly back.

Josh took a deep breath and turned his gaze to Kandria.

"What did you mean about the First coming here to Earth? Just why are you all here?"

"A perceptive question," said Kandria. "I've said before, we are bound closely to the planet. The world on which we grew, as did the Yshan people, is not just a lump of rock, it has an awareness, a life force. We are part of it, just as you are. But we had to leave when the Star died and the Aliens took over or we too would have died as the planet began dying."

"The *planet* would die?" Charlie's face showed the same enormous shock that Josh felt at those words.

Kandria nodded. "The Aliens are not new to us. They had nearly destroyed us before, an enormously evil force that we do not understand at all. They would have killed off the planet's life force, just as they are doing now. So we came to Earth, a planet much like our home planet, with its own life force in which we can survive. The Human race has also depended on that force for its survival."

All three of the young people were silent for a moment as they tried to digest this information.

"Back at the family meeting," Kyle said, "you said something about the Yshans needing the First and the First needing the Yshans. And you also said you needed the planet for your survival. You've just explained some of that, but it's time you explained the rest of it."

"Very soon," said Kandria. "First, we need to take a short trip outside. Something important is happening."

She stood up and led the way out of the room, down a corridor and opened a door at one end. The others followed her in and were astonished to see several ground vehicles parked in a garage.

Kandria saw the looks of astonishment and laughed.

"Sometimes, even The First need to go shopping!" she said. "We go into town just like any of the locals!"

They piled into a capacious station wagon with Henry sitting next to Kandria, inseparable as always and Charlie next to him in the front seat. Kyle and Josh took the back seats as the car pulled out into sunlight of a beautiful, sunny day.

Two or three kilometres along a quiet road, Kandria pointed to an attractive farmhouse a few hundred metres from the road.

"That was the Foster family home," she said. "That was where Charlie first took Kyle, Sophie and Josh horse riding and Charlie's mother realised that the twins were not human."

Charlie wiped a tear from her eyes. That story was all part of the collection of legends taught to all schoolchildren in the Yshan worlds

After a few more minutes of silence, the car drove slowly past the grounds of a school building.

"Is that..." asked Josh, fascinated.

Kandria nodded. "Yes, that's the school," she said. "Right there by the gate is where Kyle and Josh practiced their unarmed combat and where Omaron and one of his thugs attacked them to their great cost."

"Of course, you actually saw that fight!" said Josh. "You were there!"

"I was Miss Hickey, the new teacher," replied Kandria. "Sent by the Fleet Admiral to protect Kyle and Sophie against just that threat. But as it turned out, Sophie was part of the threat."

"This is incredible," said Kyle. "All these stories, they're so bound up in our history. To see the places where they happened, it's astonishing."

The three visitors stared at the building. Pictures of the school were common in the history books of the Yshan people of the new Commonwealth and this scene was well known. There were two new buildings to one side and on the other, a large greenhouse had been constructed.

"It's amazing!" said Josh. "Over a century later, it still looks much the same, just like any school anywhere else in the country!"

"And I bet the classrooms are still like they were," agreed Charlie. "Hey, look, a couple of kids! They're wearing the same uniform our namesakes wore!"

But Kandria was staring at something else. Two people were standing by the school gate, looking with concentration at the car and its occupants.

"Who are they?" asked Charlie. "They're weird! I've never seen anyone so tall!"

"We knew they'd find us some day," muttered Kandria.

"Who?" asked Kyle.

"Aliens," Kandria replied. "They've been looking for us since the invasion and they must have picked up rumours of our presence here. We first detected them a few days ago. That's why this is happening, why Henry's rebirth occurred and why I came to get you. Whatever life force of the Star remains must have detected their arrival."

"Aliens?" snapped Kyle. "Do they know who we are?"

"They know who I am, certainly," said Kandria. "So they may be able to work out who you are. We need to get back to the base."

She accelerated and drove round the corner, returning to the main road and ten minutes later they were back underground in the secret location.

"What now?" asked Kyle as they took their seats again in the room where they had been earlier. "How long before we must leave?"

"Not long," replied Kandria. "There's no doubt the aliens will report back to their base, but they can't be certain about your identities and they have no indications of where you came from. But it could be some days before they do anything about it."

"What will they do, do think?" asked Josh.

"Probably send a military squad to attack this base," replied Kandria.

"Can you defend it?" asked Kyle. "I'm pretty sure you have some good weapons."

"It's not a problem," replied Kandria with a smile.

"Then is it time to tell us how all this began and how the Star appeared?" asked Charlie.

"Indeed it is," said Kandria.

Chapter 8 - The Very Distant Past

The planet was called Yggrandal by its people. They had enjoyed many thousands of years of peace, wealth and a passion for exploring their world and learning of its mysteries and beauties.

Now it was a time of crisis.

Only months before, an alien species had appeared in their skies, in ships far advanced on the technology of Yggrandal. No communication had taken place but the aliens simply destroyed towns and cities and set up mining operations in many areas, taking minerals from the land and leaving devastation in place of beauty.

Now there was just hunger and disease as the population declined by many thousands every day.

"We are nearly at the end," said Emorill. By acclaim, he was the leader of what had once been a global government, a group selected by lottery from its adult citizens every five years.

A wave of sadness swept through the hall. The entire population of the city was here, no more than a thousand people and nobody knew how many, if any remained in the rest of the world. There had been no communications from anywhere on the planet for weeks now.

"And our world also seems to be ending," said a young woman at the front of the crowd. "When we still could talk to people all over the planet, they all told of the plants and animals dying."

A murmur of grief ran through the crowd.

"We and the planet seem to be tied together, somehow," said Emorill. "I think our planet will die when we have gone."

"And we have no idea who these aliens are or where they came from?" asked an elderly man.

Emorill shook his head. "Not from this world, that's all we know for sure. We have never seen one. They remain in their vehicles and destroy all we have ever built."

"Another world!" sighed the young woman who had spoken before. "We have dreamed of such things, told tales to our children, but how horrible that our first contact would lead to our destruction."

Silence fell in the hall. Everybody there knew that their lives were coming to an end soon. The strange ships had appeared over the city in the last two weeks and already the damage had been horrendous. The attacks were carried out without any apparent pattern, just a child's eager destruction of everything standing.

A small light appeared in the space between Emorill and the crowd. Instinctively, people moved away, giving the light more space but there seemed no fear in the room as if the light emitted a calming influence. It grew stronger and with it sounded a low, musical note like a cathedral organ playing softly.

The light seemed to spin, beams flashed out from the centre of it and then it faded. There was a huge, collective gasp as the people saw a man standing there.

"It's time we met," said the man. "There is much to do."

He looked like any man in the hall. He was of medium height, stocky build, dressed in simple attire much like everybody else and he carried a bag over his shoulders which he placed on the floor. And yet there was something about him, a power of personality that shone out over the hall and covered everybody with a protective cloak of love.

"You are right," he said, smiling at the leader, Emorill. "You and the planet are tied together. You draw on the world's inner powers for your own and at the same time, it needs you to fill its own dreams."

"Who *are* you?" croaked Emorill, the shock taking all strength from him.

"My people are those who preceded you on this world," said the man. "We lived here for nearly eight hundred thousand years, just as you have, peacefully, happily, living closely with the planet's own life force."

Emorill shook his head in confusion. All around him, the silence was complete. Every face in the room was turned to this mysterious newcomer, but there was no fear in the hall.

The man smiled in sympathy.

"This is hard for you, I know. But what I said is true. We had a full civilisation centuries before your people developed into tribes and when we saw your growth into civilisation, we knew our time to move on had also come."

Still struggling for self-control, Emorill took a deep breath. "Where did you go?" he whispered. "Another world?"

The man shook his head. "Not another world. Another dimension. Just as your people will do some day when you have fully grown and your growth will greatly exceed ours."

"I doubt we will live long enough," said Emorill sadly. "We will probably all die in the next few days."

"If that happens, then the whole world will also die, as one of you has already suggested. And if the world dies, then my people will also die, because we are still a part of this planet, just as you are."

"But how can it be stopped?" demanded Emorill. "These invaders have weapons we cannot even imagine. I think the people in this hall are the last of our kind."

The newcomer shook his head. "And now you have a weapon that will drive them away."

He bent down and opened the bag at his feet, standing up again with what looked like a crystal about the size of his head. It was white and seemed to glow slightly.

"And how will that help us?" demanded Emorill. His whole body radiated disappointment and contempt.

"This crystal contains the minds, the skills, the wisdom and the powers of all my people," replied the mysterious stranger. "First, it needs to find the person in whom it can entrust that wisdom and guide them to lead. It will take care of the aliens in its own way."

"And how will it do that?" asked Emorill, starting to sense some hope that the entire world was not coming to an end after all.

The man came closer to him and held out the crystal. "Take it," he said.

Cautiously, Emorill took the crystal from the stranger. It weighed less than he had expected and he sensed enormous power within it.

"Hold it above your head," the man commanded.

With just a pause, Emorill obeyed, uncertain of what was happening. The crystal hummed with a low note and the gleam increased just enough to be detected but beyond that, nothing strange occurred.

The man smiled and took the crystal back.

"You have been a fine leader," he said. "But you are not the one to return the people to greatness."

He turned and studied the group. In the faces before him, he saw hope, concern, happiness, even some derision. He beckoned to the young woman who had spoken before and she approached, looking nervous.

"You try," said the man, handing her the crystal and she took it gingerly. Immediately it hummed louder and the gleam from inside it grew stronger.

The man gestured at her to hold it up and she did so.

Immediately, the crystal emitted a light that seemed stronger than every sun in the skies, even the whole Galaxy. The light flooded into every corner of the hall, lit up every face and wiped out every shadow.

In the confusion, joy broke out as everybody seemed to recognise that their tragedy had been averted. When they looked around to ask the man what this meant, he had vanished.

Chapter 9

"That was over a million years ago," said Kandria, looking with amusement at the faces around her, utterly enthralled by the story she had been telling.

"But what happened then?" breathed Charlie. She had been entranced by the tale as it unfolded.

"The aliens vanished within weeks," replied Kandria. "It was almost like a long-ago story here on Earth about how the Martians invaded and almost destroyed Earth but fell sick to all of the planet's microbes and germs because they had no immunity. We found no dead specimens, they simply vanished. But our people recovered, began to expand again and as they did, the planet too recovered. The young woman for whom the crystal had glowed remained a leader for over a century. We were already a long-lived race, and we expanded our normal life-times to over two thousand years. And we began to expand outward, too. We had so many of the ships left by the aliens that we were able to develop them for our own use and later design our own space-ships and slowly we built a planetary empire."

"So why are you not still there?" asked Josh. "What happened to you?"

"Did you see the similarity between our tale of getting the crystal and the same legends that the Yshan people have?" asked Kandria.

"Ah! Of course!" said Kyle. "It contained the minds and wisdom of your predecessors. So is that the same crystal that was given to us?"

Kandria shook her head.

"We had the same story as our earlier race. We began to grow out of our physical bodies and into a new dimension. In the last few years of our time on the planet, our crystal began to fade and finally died. The one we gave you contained the same wisdom and minds of most of our own people and there are few of us left now. In time, the same will happen to the Yshan race."

"Kandria," broke in Charlie. "What did you mean about the planet having dreams and a life force? How can a planet be *alive?*"

"Ours is," replied Kandria. "Many planets around the universe are living entities, just as Earth is and the people living on it are part of the life force. If they die, the planet dies and the reverse is also true."

"And the alien presence is killing our world?" asked Charlie.

Kandria nodded. "That is so. The two races are utterly dangerous to each other and it looks like they found their own Star to use as a weapon."

"But our Star is dead!" interjected Kyle.

"And that's why you are here," replied Kandria. "Now it's time for you to prepare to return home with the Emperor and the Star."

"A new Star?" asked Josh. "Are we going to get a new Star somehow?"

Kandria merely smiled, stood up and walked out of the room. The rest of them followed, puzzled.

She led them back to the large hall where they had first arrived. It seemed that the rest of her people were also there. She stopped by the table where they had eaten breakfast earlier, but it was completely clear and shone with a polished wood surface.

"Put your medallions on the table," Kandria said. "Henry, yours too."

The little boy reached inside his shirt and pulled out another medallion identical to the three carried by Josh, Charlie and Kyle. All of them were glowing strongly. Gently, Kandria nudged them until they were touching.

The medallions began to glow more strongly and increased the energy until it was hard to look directly at them.

The gleam became a ball of light over each medallion which expanded until with a soundless flicker, all four sources of light combined as one and then it was too bright to look at. The three friends hid their eyes until they sensed the power of the light had faded and they dropped their hands from their faces.

Sitting on the table, humming gently was a Star.

* * * *

All four of them stared at the glowing crystal for several moments.

Josh was the first to look away to make a comment to Kandria but what he saw made him gasp with shock.

Apart from his two friends and the little boy called Henry, the room was empty.

"Where is everybody?" exclaimed Charlie, looking

around in bewilderment. "I didn't see anyone leave."

Kyle was smiling with joy. He moved to the table and began stroking his fingertips over the Star. It glowed a little more strongly and hummed, almost like a cat purring.

"They're in here!" he said and picked it up. He turned to the little boy.

"Henry," he said. "I think you know what to do."

"Yes," said the child, the first word he had spoken since they had met him just a few hours before. He lifted the Star above his head.

The light of all the stars in the entire Galaxy seemed to shine from the crystal and illuminated every corner of the huge room.

"Time to go home," said Kyle. "The Emperor must reclaim his Empire."

Chapter 10

"These will completely immobilise the alien ships," said the Chief Engineer at the Gregory Foster Institute of Technology. The building was not huge, though much of it was underground for safety reasons. It was named after the father of the first Charlie Foster, a human who displayed extraordinary genius after being introduced to Yshan science and took it further than anyone could have dreamed.

Commander Kyle Yshan looked at the small torpedo in its frame. It was nothing remarkable in appearance, about a metre long, quite broad and looked more like the pictures Kyle had seen of the blimps used for advertising back on Earth. It was a featureless black with nothing obvious to be seen on the outside.

"How does it do that?" asked Kyle doubtfully.

The engineer laughed. "We've been busy while you've been holidaying back on Earth, Commander," he said. "We stripped down the alien ship to every nut and bolt, analysed every computerised part, tested every printed circuit and then did it all again!"

"And did you find out how they'd neutralised the effect of our earlier torpedoes?"

The engineer grinned smugly. He was a tall, middle-aged man with a full head of red hair, an equally bushy, red moustache and the broad-shouldered, lanky build of an athlete, spoiled by a small pot belly under his white laboratory coat.

"We certainly did! They'd developed a doo-hickey that generated a force field that blanked out the ones our torpedoes developed. It was dead easy to build something that would counter that effect."

"And that is what's in the torpedo now?" asked Kyle.

The engineer blew a noisy raspberry. "That would be MUCH too easy," he said. "Give us some credit, Commander, my team is made up of the best theoretical physicists, mathematicians and cosmologists in the Commonwealth. We had that little problem cleared up in a day, so we went quite a bit further."

"And?" inquired Kyle. The engineer's enthusiasm and air of hidden secrets was interesting him. What else did this man have?

"We also looked at the fuel sources," said the other man. "They're a very potent mixture of energy cells and nuclear power that provide enormous energy but tends to be unstable. So they stabilise the mixture with a blanket force field that works very well."

Kyle laughed out loud as he saw where the man was going. "And you found a way of cancelling that force field?"

"We surely did," shouted the engineer, his delight too much to keep under control. "Put one of these babies within a million kilometres of one of their ships and not only will all their systems fail, but their internal power sources will get so unstable, everybody on board will be too occupied trying to stop themselves blowing up to think about fighting!"

Kyle's grin was almost ear to ear. "That's fantastic!" he said. "How soon can you get them into production?"

"Starting today," the engineer replied with a satisfied smile. "We'll have several thousand within a year."

"Your team has certainly earned its keep," said Kyle.

"Like I said, Commander, we're the very best there is. There's more than I've told you."

"Good grief, isn't that enough? You've given us the weapon to defeat those aliens, just like the first Gregory Foster did. What else did you do?"

"We ripped into their navigation system. What we found is the perfect addition to the torpedo mechanisms. We found a transponder system that shows us the location of every ship in their fleet. That's very useful of course, so we built into the torpedo, a system of finding each ship and flying straight there through the nearest wormhole and any others in between. Commander, we can put a torpedo next to every ship in their fleet and we know exactly how many ships they have and where they are."

"How many have you got ready?" asked Kyle.

"Just four," replied the engineer.

"Have they been tested?"

"Not against a real life alien warship," the engineer replied.

"Get them aboard my ship," said Kyle. He touched his communicator.

"Admiral, it's time to go hunting," he said.

Chapter 11 – Alien Hunting

"Report," said Commander Kyle Yshan from his Command Seat on the bridge of his frigate, the Planetary Commonwealth Ship, *"Charlie Foster"* which had just soared through a wormhole after leaving home base eight hours before.

"On target, sir," replied Lieutenant Josh Bradshaw from the pilot's seat. "We're in the Home Galaxy, Sector MPR057, 82,000 light years from Yshan Home World."

"Location of our target?" demanded Kyle.

"Still registering in Sector KLJ098," replied the Navigation Officer who had been given the task of monitoring the system taken from the captured alien battle cruiser. "That's one wormhole transit away, so there's no way we can be detected."

Kyle knew all the data, having developed the battle plan himself but going through the procedures of "Challenge and Verification" as it was known was a security measure and one that enabled all the crew to follow the action.

"Weapons?" said Kyle.

"Weapons, aye," replied a voice through the communications speaker. The Weapons Officer was down in the torpedo room.

"Status?" asked Kyle.

"All four fish armed and ready," replied the Weapons Officer. "The first one is programmed to pass through the wormhole and meet the alien in its present position."

"Thanks, Weapons," replied Kyle. "Nav, ready to follow?"

"Ready, sir," said the Navigations Officer.

"Twenty seconds after the torpedo goes, follow," ordered Kyle.

"Twenty seconds, aye," replied Nav.

"Weapons, first fish, shoot!"

"On its way, sir," said the voice from the torpedo room.

The Bridge was silent as they watched the forward screen. The massive, flaming ring of the wormhole erupted into life as the torpedo raced through and then it faded. In dead silence the officers waited as the countdown continued, then the engines thundered into life and the *"Charlie Foster"* accelerated sharply and went through the wormhole in the identical direction and at the same speed as the torpedo.

"Position!" snapped Kyle.

"Sector KLJ098 on target," replied Nav. "We are less than one million kilometres from the recorded position of the alien cruiser and closing. I have no sign of it, so it's probably cloaked."

"And the fish?"

"Torpedo should ignite in five, four, three, two, one... there she blows!"

In the black distance, a tiny gleam lit up and faded again. In the background of stars, a small circle blacked out a patch of the galaxy's light.

"Its cloaking mechanism has gone," said the Navigation Officer. He couldn't keep the excitement out of his voice. "It's just three hundred thousand kilometres away."

"Stand by regular torpedoes," ordered Kyle. "We don't know if their weapons have been disabled. Josh, take us towards that ship. Be prepared for anything."

"Aye, sir," replied Josh in the pilot's seat.

"Anything showing, Number One?" asked Kyle to his First Officer sitting to his right.

"Checking, sir," she said softly, her eyes intent on the instruments on the small screen beside her. Then she grinned. "They're dead in the water, Skipper," she said. "Nothing's working over there!"

"Keep heading there, Josh," said Kyle. "Everybody, they may look dead, but..."

As he spoke, the space ahead lit up in a furious explosion of energy. The ball of fire expanded to fill the screens and they automatically darkened to protect the eyes of the watchers.

The fire subsided and the screen lightened up again.

"Nothing there, sir," reported the First Officer. "Just dust and a few small bits of debris. It looks like their nuclear cells blew up."

"That destabiliser doo-hickey worked pretty well, then," murmured Kyle. "The engineer will be delighted."

He pressed the communicator button and the face of Fleet Admiral Josh Bradshaw appeared.

"We have a weapon, sir," said Kyle. "The battle cruiser blew up as we approached. It needed just one torpedo."

The relief on the Admiral's face was obvious.

"Well done, everybody," he said. "So the weapon worked and it looks like the alien computer gives us the location of every one of their ships."

"I've got three fish left, sir."

"Happy hunting, Kyle," said the Admiral.

"Thank you, sir," said Kyle. "Navigator? Where's the next alien ship?"

"Two wormhole transits, Skipper, Sector AQJ910. There are two cruisers together."

"Two together, eh?" said Kyle. "Too juicy a target to miss. Feed the coordinates to Weapons, Lieutenant. Weapons, tell me when you have the next two torpedoes programmed."

"Coordinates received, we'll be ready in three minutes."

"I think my long-ago ancestor in that war back on Earth would have said, "Tally Ho!" said Josh. "It's what the fighter pilots said when they saw the enemy aircraft."

"Then Tally Ho it is, Josh!" Kyle could not keep the excitement out of his voice and the atmosphere on the Bridge reflected it.

"Time to reclaim the Empire, then?" asked Josh.

"Time to reclaim the Empire," agreed Kyle.

* * * *

On the bridge of the Pfor'Xscur Battle Cruiser, the scene was peaceful. The twin to this cruiser was also in orbit round their home world, just a hundred kilometres away and clearly visible as it moved out of the planet's night shadow and into sunlight.

"Freighters report all loads deposited on the surface, Captain," said the First Officer.

"Good," replied the Captain, stirring in his seat after some hours of watching the convoy of freighters they had escorted from Yshan Home World. "Navigator, set course for base."

A few minutes of silence reigned on the bridge as the ship got under way.

"These convoys are starting to bore me, Number One," said the captain. "We're a warship, and all we do is escort those freighters from that miserable Yshan Planet and back again."

The First Officer didn't smile. "Our people need the minerals we take, sir."

The Captain sighed. "I know, I know, but it's boring all the same. It's not as if the old Yshan fleet still exists and they all seem to have vanished anyway. We're getting rusty like this!"

"I'm not so sure," replied the other officer. "Those reports of one of our ships simply vanishing last year still worry me. They said they were chasing an Yshan frigate and then they disappeared. What could have caused that?"

The Captain shrugged. "More likely their control systems for their fuel cells failed and the ship blew up. Believe me, there's no Yshan Fleet anywhere in the Universe."

At that moment, the lights went out and were immediately replaced by the dim red glow of the emergency back-up lights.

"Report!" shouted the Captain.

"All systems failed," came the voice from the Engineering Deck. "Propulsion is down, life support is down, weapons are down."

"How! How can that happen? Get onto it, get those systems fixed!" The Captain was displaying panic. He was right, over a century of their dominance over the old Yshan Empire had provided not a single need for emergency action at all and they had lost the capacity to deal with it. Even though the mystery of the complete disappearance of the Cruiser many months ago had caused worry in the High Command and there had been not a clue as to the cause of it, nothing else had disturbed the Pfor'Xscur Empire since its successful invasion of the Yshan Galactic Empire and the total disappearance of the Yshan Imperial Fleet.

The panic-stricken voice from Engineering came back on the speaker.

"Sir! Fuel stabilisation has failed. We need to get out of here!"

The Captain decided immediately. "Abandon Ship!" he called. "Abandon Ship!"

That was as far as he got. At that moment, the cruiser was blown into cosmic dust as the fuel systems blew up like a dozen nuclear bombs.

The crew didn't know that the other cruiser a short distance away exploded in the same manner just two seconds later.

Chapter 12

"It's all very confusing," said the tall young man with fair hair. He looked to be in his late twenties.

"I know intellectually that I'm less than two years old, or at least, this *body* is less than two years old," he continued. "But I remember my entire life before, first as Henry then as Emperor Garamax, everything, that is, up to the moment when I died on the ship returning from Earth. The fact that I was murdered by Sophie over a hundred and twenty years ago, that's the thing I have so much difficult grasping."

"I don't think we can have any idea of what you've gone through," said Kyle. "Is there anything we can do?"

Henry smiled. "The Star is giving me a fast education on the history since my murder, so I'm up to date! But Charlie, Josh and Kyle were my best friends back then and they look so much like you do now, I feel you really are the same people."

"But I don't look anything like the original Charlie Foster!" protested Charlie. "I'm a Bradshaw, not a direct descendant of hers at all!"

"Strange, isn't it?" said Henry. "I think my mind is convincing me that you *do* look like her, even though I can see the difference when I look at pictures of the first Charlie. Anyway, it doesn't matter! You three are my friends!"

"And that's our honour," said Josh. "But now we have to get home to our original planet and restore your Empire."

Henry grimaced. "I think the important thing is to get rid of those appalling aliens and restore a decent life for everybody."

"That first," agreed Kyle. "And we need to bring the Empress Sophie to trial. I wonder if she really is the original one?"

"I think so," said Josh. "Omaron Yshan is already looking about sixty years old and aging fast. That Dark Star must be the reason why they stayed so young but now that he's away from its influence, it can't keep him that way."

"Couldn't happen to a nicer man," said Kyle with a grin.

The buzzer on his collar gave a tiny grunt. Kyle listened briefly to a voice in his ear and looked at Josh. Informality was gone, military discipline returned.

"Time to get on board, Lieutenant Bradshaw," he said. "We're off to war."

"Yes, sir," replied Josh.

"And of course I'm coming too," said Galactic Emperor Garamax 19th.

"Of course, Sire," said Kyle. "Your Imperial Fleet is waiting for you."

Chapter 13

"This is the Captain," said Commander Kyle Yshan.

The frigate, the *"Charlie Foster"* hung in space at the very edge of the home galaxy that had been governed by the Yshan Royal Family before the invasion by the alien fleet over a hundred and twenty years ago. Just a few kilometres away, the flagship of the Fleet, the *"Admiral Sestucal"* floated silently, surrounded by many other ships. Aboard the flagship was the Fleet Admiral and with him, the young man who once was the Galactic Emperor and soon would be again.

Within a sealed case was the gleaming crystal, the new Star of the Yshan Kings.

"Time to give you the battle plan briefing," continued Kyle.

* * * *

Back in the basements of the Gregory Foster Institute of Technology, the atmosphere was tense but not worried. The scene was much like some pictures that hung on the walls of the old control rooms during the space exploration days on old Earth, nearly two hundred years before, lines of men and women at control screens.

"Each of those one hundred positions is controlling ten torpedoes," said the Chief Engineer, the man who had briefed Kyle Yshan on the capabilities of the new torpedoes. The silent woman standing with him was Charlotte Bradshaw, the elderly sister of the Fleet Admiral and the great aunt of the pilot aboard Kyle's frigate.

"As you know, the captured alien battle cruiser gave us their computers which among all the other wonderful data also gave us the ability to track every single ship in their fleet. We've coded each torpedo with the coordinates of a ship and they are scattered all over their own galaxy and the Yshan galaxy, with only a small fleet surrounding the original Yshan home planet."

"How many ships in all?" asked the elder Charlie.

"Twelve hundred and thirty," replied the engineer. "Of those, three hundred are near the home planet. Our own fleet is six hundred ships and they are armed with six torpedoes each."

"So what's going to happen?" asked the elderly woman. She was ten years older than the Admiral but like her brother, full of energy and equipped with a powerful brain. She was, in fact, the top mathematician at the Institute and had played a significant part in designing the new torpedoes.

"It's all in the timing," said the engineer. "Those people at their terminals have already launched their torpedoes and right now, the computers are plotting the exact positions of each of the alien ships and the time taken for the torpedoes to reach their wormholes and then the target ships. They will all have to be despatched at different times to hit their targets at exactly the same moment. So a thousand torpedoes have targeted all the alien ships that are away from the home planet."

"And the fleet around the home planet?" asked Charlie.

"Same thing. Our fleet will fire their torpedoes at their own targets and go through the wormholes and arrive around the home planet all at the same moment. Every alien ship should be destroyed within a second or two of each other."

"And it's all up to the computers now, is it?"

"Yes it is. Things should start happening in about twenty minutes."

The two senior scientists shook hands.

"See you back on Home World of the new Yshan Empire," said Charlie.

"You bet!" said the engineer.

*　*　*　*

"So it's all up to the computers," said Kyle, finishing his briefing to the crew. "The fleet will move through the wormhole and make three more jumps through further wormholes to arrive at Home World, all automatically controlled by the computers. We will release our torpedoes at exactly the same moment all the torpedoes controlled on the ground at the Institute basement will hit theirs located away from Home World. We will follow the torpedoes through the final wormhole and arrive at Home World a few seconds after the torpedoes have struck. We have nearly twice as many ships as the aliens and we have six torpedoes each, with one programmed to a specific target, in our case a frigate about the same size as us, and two others programmed to alternate targets. The rest can be fired should we need them for any other convenient target we may see or as back-ups for the others. So man your stations, monitor everything and be prepared to take manual control in case anything goes wrong. We'll be moving off in about fifteen minutes. To your stations, everybody."

All around the ship, the crew of thirty-three officers and men and women went calmly about their duties. If any of them showed nerves or fear, the well-disciplined professionals hid it, taking their lead from the complete composure of their Captain and Bridge Officers.

The Weapons team checked their new torpedoes again, checked their conventional high-explosive torpedoes should they be needed and made sure there were no loose objects that could fly around and cause damage in the event of high-stress manoeuvres.

The Navigator checked for the tenth time that he had the coordinates of their first, second and third alternate targets and that they had been correctly fed to the Weapons team.

Josh tested his controls that he'd had modified by the ship's engineer to resemble the controls of a conventional fighter plane of an earlier age back on Earth. He'd become so hooked on the fighter techniques of that time and of the war in which his ancestor had flown a Hurricane that he felt more comfortable and more in control with the old "stick and rudder" system than with the standard methods. Also linked to his control were the massive cannons that fired explosive shells, a weapon very rarely used.

Kyle sat calmly in his Captains chair, sipping at a mug of coffee. His stomach was churning and he was sure that was true of everybody else aboard the ship, but keeping a calm, controlled air was essential for a ship's Captain.

"Fleet's moving, sir," said the First Officer softly. "First wormhole transit in eight minutes."

Kyle touched the ship-wide communications button on his seat's arm.

"All right, everybody, we're moving. We'll be in action very soon. Like our young pilot says, "Tally Ho!" and let's get those aliens out of our home."

Chapter 14

Within seconds the entire fleet had passed through the wormhole, the first of three between their position and the final lap to the home planet.

"On target, in sector, KLS871," reported the Navigator. "The fleet is together. Next wormhole in fourteen minutes."

Nobody had anything to do except monitor their equipment. The entire flight was controlled by computer as the complete fleet had to arrive in the final sector and fire their torpedoes within fractions of a second of each other, just as the torpedoes being controlled back at the Technical Institute had to meet their targets in the aliens' home galaxy simultaneously to avoid those ships giving the alarm before they were destroyed.

"Next wormhole transit, on my mark, twenty seconds," reported the Navigation Officer.

Kyle nodded to signify he had heard. His throat felt dry and he didn't feel like speaking.

The ring of fire erupted ahead and the fleet went soaring through.

"On target, in sector, VBS650," reported the Navigator. "The fleet is together. Next wormhole in twenty-one minutes."

Kyle tensed a little. The computers had programmed a torpedo to be released by each ship and go through the last wormhole twenty seconds ahead of the fleet. If all went to plan, the fleet would find nothing but debris when they arrived, but Kyle remembered something that had been taught at the Fleet Academy.

"A battle plan lasts only until the first shot has been fired."

"Torpedo away," reported the Navigation Officer. A few seconds later, the fire ring of the wormhole burst into life.

"Ten seconds," said the Navigation Officer hoarsely, not able to control the nerves completely.

"Battle Stations," ordered Kyle and the sirens went off to alert the entire crew.

The fire ring approached and the screen showed a number of other ships of the fleet already going through on their computer-controlled paths and then the *"Charlie Foster"* was through as well.

The space on the other side of the wormhole was utter chaos. Debris lay everywhere and without the protective shields, collisions with huge chunks of metal would have destroyed the frigate in seconds.

Kyle couldn't help the overwhelming shock he felt. The scene of devastation reminded him that more than three hundred ships had been destroyed and with them their crews. Kyle had no love for the species that had invaded his Empire and treated the citizens of the Yshan Galaxy with such cruelty, but still... several thousand intelligent beings had just died and he could not avoid feeling the horror.

"Sir! Incoming!" shouted the First Officer as the screen showed a tiny spark approaching the frigate. Kyle had no time to call to Josh for evasive action but Josh didn't need the order. The engines bellowed into life under intense acceleration and the frigate rolled over and dived sharply, rolled again and climbed back, reversed direction and pointed at the source of the enemy torpedo which had flashed by, missing the frigate by a hundred metres and disappearing.

"You have control, Josh," said Kyle belatedly.

There was no reply from the pilot. He was busily hauling the ship into a tight loop that would have crushed the crew had it not been for the gravity controls.

"There it is!" reported the First Officer. "Its shields must be down, but somehow one of the torpedoes didn't function properly. It's still alive."

"Got it," said Josh more to himself. He centred the alien ship in his sights and flung the *"Charlie Foster"* at the target. At the last second, the enemy ship rolled tightly and pulled away, looped upward and tried to come in behind the frigate.

"This bloke's good!" muttered Josh. "We seem to be in an actual dogfight!"

He rolled rapidly, several times and then pulled down in an inverted loop, rolled again and pulled back up, slapped the throttles shut and the enemy ship raced underneath him, clearly confused by the manoeuvre. Josh pushed the stick forward, brought the enemy vessel back into his sights and closed up to within just a few hundred metres.

The other ship desperately threw itself around, trying to shake the frigate off its tail, but Josh concentrated fiercely, gradually reducing the distance between the two, not at all aware of the dead silence on the bridge as everybody watched this incredible battle.

Josh took one hand off the throttle and touched his gun control. Four immensely powerful cannons roared, their sound audible on the bridge. Streaks of red tracer shells hurtled toward the enemy ship and then in a soundless blast it blew itself into dust.

"Gotcha!" said Josh and pulled the ship around the explosion.

Kyle realised he hadn't taken a breath for some time and relaxed with an explosive gasp, echoed by almost every other person on the bridge.

"Great flying, Josh," he said, trying to calm the thumping of his heart.

Josh didn't answer. He had slumped down in his seat, clearly drained by the sudden demands that had been placed on him.

"Medic to the Bridge!" called Kyle and nodded at his First Officer. "Take over Josh's place, will you, Number One? Locate the flagship and get us alongside."

Two officers pulled Josh from his seat and laid him out on the floor as a medical officer arrived and began to examine him.

"The Admiral on fleet broadcast," reported the Navigation Officer as the Admiral's face appeared on the screen. He looked sombre.

"I can report the complete destruction of the alien fleet," the older man said, his voice reflecting tension and fatigue. "Not only here around Home World, but the Institute has reported total success with the remotely fired torpedoes. There is not a single enemy ship left in action. Not all of them blew up but all of them have lost their propulsion and weapons systems and the crews have had to evacuate and take refuge on any possible planets nearby as their life support systems also failed."

The old man had to stop and wipe tears from his eyes.

"I am about to take Emperor Garamax 19th down to the home world," he continued. "Commander Kyle

Yshan, please have Lieutenant Bradshaw and yourself join us."

"You bet sir," muttered Kyle, so softly that the Admiral couldn't hear him.

"The Lieutenant is fine, sir," reported the medical office attending Josh. "But that episode drained him like a squeezed sponge! He's fit and strong, give him twenty minutes or so."

Behind him, Josh was sitting up and looking around. His face was white.

Kyle let out a laugh. "Your however-many-greats grandfather back on Earth would have been proud of you, Josh!" he said. "That was superb flying!"

"It just goes to show you, sir," said Josh. "Some things never change, but who would have thought a fighter pilot of two hundred years ago would have shown us how to defeat an enemy space-ship?"

"Get yourself ready, Lieutenant Bradshaw," said Kyle. "We have a date with an Empress."

Chapter 15 - The Empress Sophie

A fleet of thirty-two shuttlecraft descended to the city that had once been the Capital of the Yshan Galactic Empire. One of them contained the Admiral, Josh, Kyle and Charlie who had finally persuaded the Admiral to let her come along. It also contained Emperor Garamax 19th who had been on the throne of the Yshan Empire until murdered by his cousin Sophie when the aliens had invaded and placed her on the throne instead.

The Emperor, now fully restored in appearance to the tall, handsome young man with a charismatic face that he had been, stood before the viewing screen gazing out at the city. His hand rested on the metal case that held the Star.

The view outside was not impressive. The city had been allowed to degenerate over the century or more that the aliens had ruled and the buildings and roads all showed the decay.

As the final shuttle touched down, the Admiral rose to his feet.

"Send out the troops first," he said. "The enemy may still be around and I want no more shocks."

The shuttle pilot, a Captain of the fleet nodded and spoke briefly into his communications system. The doors to the other shuttles opened and armed troops raced out or drove out on armoured personnel carriers. They began dispersing through the city while two large groups made for the Royal Palace. Four armed men in full battle equipment stayed in the shuttle.

The Fleet Captain remained at his position in the pilot's chair, listening intently to the reports from his troops.

"No sign of the enemy at all, sir," he said at one point. "The Palace detail has now entered the building. No sign of life at all."

"Thank you, Captain," said the Admiral.

Another ten minutes passed before the Captain spoke again.

"Civilians, sir!" he said. "They've started coming out of the buildings. Our men are telling them what's happened."

"Any reactions?" asked the Admiral.

The Captain turned to him and smiled. "They seem relieved!" he said.

The others in the shuttle laughed.

"It's time for me to get to the Palace," said Henry and picked up the metal case.

The Admiral gestured at the armed troops who walked out of the shuttle. Kyle heard the sound of another hatch opening and two ground cars appeared in front of the doorway.

"Let me go out first, Sire," the Admiral said and led the way outside. He stared around the immediate environment and looked back at the pilot with a question in his face.

"No alien life forms detected, sir," said the Captain.

The Admiral nodded and waited for the others to come out.

Henry took a seat in the second car together with Josh, Kyle and Charlie while the Admiral took the leading vehicle with his troops and they began heading for the Palace.

"How strange this is," said Henry. "I know I have never been here before, but I know it so well. This is my home."

"I hope it's in better shape than the city," said Kyle.

"I imagine the Empress has at least kept her own place in luxury," said Charlie. Her tone was sarcastic. The other men grinned at her.

A low rumble like a distant storm ran around the city. It seemed to vibrate even the ground under their feet.

"What on earth is that?" said Josh, puzzled. "The weather forecast said nothing about thunderstorms."

"They must be wrong," said Charlie. "The sky is getting dark."

They looked up at the sky as what appeared to be a major thunder storm was brewing.

"That's no ordinary storm," said Josh. "The sky is green!"

He was right. The sky had turned a sickly green colour while around it streamers of red raced from horizon to horizon and massive lightning strikes hit the ground in all direction.

At the same time, the ground shook and one or two buildings ahead of them seemed to wave like trees in a wind.

"This isn't an earthquake zone," called Kyle, barely heard above the howling wind that had sprung up and the crack of the lightning bolts. "What's going on?"

"The box!" shouted Henry in panic. "It's burning hot!"

"Out!" commanded Kyle. "Something dangerous is happening."

They hurriedly left the car, not before Kyle saw the box containing the Star glowing bright red with huge surges of energy.

The car ahead had also stopped and the four armed men surrounded Henry to protect him.

The storm increased in intensity. There was no rain, but massive bolts of energy thundered to the ground, mostly aimed at the Palace. The building began to glow with an eerie yellow light until the whole Palace was covered.

"That looks like a force field," said Kyle.

A titanic explosion went off some way above them and a thunderbolt struck the ground just a hundred metres away shook the ground. All of them were blown off their feet and for a moment they were unable to breathe as the explosion had blasted all the air away. New air rushed in, making a small typhoon that blew them around like dolls for a second or two before subsiding.

The soldiers gathered round Henry, weapons ready, but there was no sign of hostile forces.

Kyle jumped to his feet, checked Henry first and then with huge relief saw that everybody was safe. He helped Charlie to her feet and she smiled at him.

"I'm fine," she said.

That lifted his spirits and he looked out to the Palace.

"That's still standing," he said.

But even as he said it, a monstrous bolt of lightning struck the Palace and the yellow glow faded. Within seconds the storm faded and the sky cleared.

"What the...? muttered Kyle. He looked back into the car and saw that the metal box appeared to have returned to normal. In sudden fear, he opened it and stared down at the Star. It appeared to be glowing a lot more brightly than before and it was humming loudly. He realised Henry was standing next to him.

"It seems okay," Kyle said and saw that Henry was smiling.

"It should be," Henry said. "It's won."

Before Kyle could ask what he meant by that, the Admiral spoke.

"We have to get to the Palace," he said. "The troops there say we have to see something. They seem very excited."

A few moments later, they entered the Palace grounds through a massive gate that had been opened by the troops. The cars stopped before the main entrance at the base of a flight of stone steps and the occupants got out.

"I'll carry the Star," said Henry and pulled the box out of the car. He refused Kyle's offer to carry it and advanced on the steps. "I remember this so well," he said. "We came out this way for my Coronation."

Admiral Bradshaw approached him, walking rapidly.

"Sire, we have to get to the Chamber of the Star," said the Admiral. "I have no idea where that is."

"This way," replied Henry with a broad smile and led the way along several corridors, walking with confidence. He stopped before a massive door at least three metres high and looking as solid as a bank vault.

"The royal quarters," he said and pointed down to a doorway at the end of one such corridor. "My apartment," he said and pointed at the huge door next to them. "This is where the Star is kept."

He touched the door which swung open soundlessly. Inside was a block of black basalt about a metre on all sides. Several armed men stood along the walls of the room, but what held everybody's attention was the basalt block and what lay on it.

It looked like shards of black glass.

"It's the Dark Star," said Henry. "I think that storm was the two Stars fighting it out."

"It shattered when that huge bolt hit the Palace," said a young officer in combat gear, one of those in the room. "And the storm stopped at just that moment."

Henry put the metal box down on the floor, opened it and raised the Star. There was a gasp of awe from the troops in the chamber. A Star had been part of Yshan legends for five thousand years and few people ever saw it. The last time one had been seen by the people was at Henry's Coronation over a hundred and twenty years before and then it had died.

"Can somebody clean that up?" Henry asked.

Several people, including Josh and Kyle and the troopers began picking up the shards of black glass or just brushing them to the floor with their arms until the surface was clear.

Henry placed the Star on the basalt block and stood back.

"About time," he said. "I'm sorry it took so long but we'll start clearing up right away."

He turned away and left the Chamber, followed by the rest and the door swung closed behind the last soldier to leave.

"It's safe," he said in reply to the Admiral's unspoken question. "The Star knows who to let in and who to keep out. Now, let's see who's in my apartment."

He began to walk down to the far door with Josh, Charlie and Kyle beside him, but he didn't have to move far because the door opened and a figure emerged.

Kyle's first reaction was admiration. The woman was quite beautiful, a pale, aristocratic face with long black hair down her back. She wore a stylish white dress with no ornamentation at all.

She stared at the group watching her and Kyle changed his views about her beauty. There was a mean, ugly look about her, an air of barely suppressed fury. She stared at each of the group in turn, her gaze passing over the soldiers and the Admiral without interest, but her glare at Charlie was intense before passing onto Josh. Then she gasped in amazement and went white.

"Josh?" she whispered, shock in her face. "How can this be?" Her gaze moved onto Kyle and this time the shock made her stumble. "This isn't possible," she mumbled as if her mouth had frozen. "My brother died many years ago. You too, Josh, you cannot be here. This is impossible."

"And do you remember me, Sophie?" said Henry softly.

The Empress Sophie stared at him, her eyes widened even more and then she collapsed to the floor.

* * * *

"Quite a severe shock, but I've given her a sedative," said the doctor. "She'll be fine, Sire."

"Thank you, doctor but stay with us, please," replied Henry.

The doctor nodded and retreated to the back of the room.

They were in what had been Henry's personal apartment until it had been taken over by Sophie after she had been installed as Empress. Sophie sat, half lying in one armchair while Henry, Kyle, Charlie and Josh sat in a half circle around her. The Admiral sat at the back of the room and several armed guards remained outside in case of any surprises.

The silence lasted another two or three minutes while they waited for Sophie to recover. Over an hour had passed since her collapse into a dead faint and Kyle had already thought that she was looking older than when she had first appeared.

Sophie stirred and sat up. She took a few deep breaths before looking up at the others watching her.

"Kyle, it *can't* be you," she whispered.

Kyle looked calmly back at her. "Quite correct, Sophie. Your brother was my great grandfather."

"But you look so like him," she continued, her voice low and croaky. "You too, Josh, you haven't changed at all," she added.

"Several generations have passed," said Josh. "But you seem to have stayed young."

Sophie didn't seem to hear him. She was staring at Charlie. She seemed also to be deliberately ignoring Henry.

"Who's this?" she demanded.

Charlie gave a small, cold smile. "Who else could I be but Charlie?" she replied.

"At least you don't look like her," said Sophie.

"We're not related," said Charlie.

Sophie sat up straight. Kyle was sure of it now, she was looking a lot older than a couple of hours ago.

"I demand to see my Uncle Omaron," she said, struggling to put authority into her words.

"Difficult," replied Kyle. "Omaron is in a cell back on the new capital world. He's aging very fast and not likely to last much longer."

Sophie's eyes widened in fear. "He's... aging?" she whispered.

"As are you, Sophie," said Kyle deliberately.

Sophie gasped as if in pain. She jumped to her feet and ran to a full-length mirror on one wall. When she saw her image, she let out a small scream and put her hands to her face.

"This can't be," she rasped. "The Star promised..."

"Your Dark Star is dead, Sophie," said Henry. "Yshan has a new Star, your allies have been destroyed. This is the end for you."

Slowly, Sophie walked back to her seat and almost fell into it. Kyle was certain of it now, she had aged at least twenty years in the last hour. Her hair no longer had the perfect sheen of youth and her complexion was developing lines that had not been there before.

Finally, she looked at Henry.

"I don't understand," she whispered. "The Emperor had no family, how could you be descended from him?"

"I'm not. I'm the original."

She shook her head in bewilderment. "No, that's not possible, I...."

"You killed me?" said Henry softly. "Yes, you did, cousin Sophie."

"Then how...?"

"The Golden Mask. Remember the Golden Mask? Nobody ever understood that strange ceremony of having the mask take the shape of the new Emperor's face. But it took my cells, my memories and it stayed in touch with my mind to make a new copy of me. Do you know I'm only three years old? But I have every memory right up to my death, including meeting you on Earth the first time, how I beat you at chess and how you threw such a tantrum because of it."

Sophie's face was white and she looked ill.

"What now?" she managed to say.

"The Yshan people have suffered for over a century under your appalling rule," said Henry. "They need to see that it's over."

He beckoned the young officer with the troops to come over.

"Take Princess Sophie Yshan into custody," he said. "Lead her outside and place her in an open vehicle and drive her slowly to the military headquarters, if that still exists."

"It does, Sire. We checked," replied the officer.

"Good," said Henry. "Make it a long, circuitous trip so as many people as possible get to see her. Arrange a press conference for all media and announce that the Princess will stand trial for treason. Keep her in a cell there, show scenes of her on the media frequently. She gets no special treatment, no extra comforts, no food other than regular prisoners' rations. The people will see her as nothing but a common criminal. I'm sure that will please them and convince them that a new life is starting for them."

The young man moved over to Sophie and held

her arm, making her stand up. He waved over two soldiers and they held her up as they led her out of the room. She seemed stooped, not the slender, erect young woman they had met such a short time ago.

"I don't think she'll last long enough for a trial," said Josh.

"Probably not," agreed Henry. "But the important thing is that the people see her arrested, in prison and nothing like the beautiful Empress of the last century of so."

"That sounds good," said Kyle.

Henry grinned like a little boy then turned to the Admiral.

"Admiral," he said. "We need to start rebuilding. We need an interim civilian government until elections can be held. I want you to arrange huge food supplies from our previous home and get engineers, medical people, teachers, everything we need to rebuild our civilisation..."

The two men moved away and out of earshot and the room gradually cleared as everybody began their new duties.

Charlie turned to Josh, a small flush on her face. "Little brother, can't you find things to do somewhere else?"

Josh looked at her and smiled. "I'm sure this heroic Fleet Pilot can find work out there," he said and waved cheerfully at the other two as he walked out.

Charlie and Kyle looked at each other.

"You're a very impressive Ship's Captain, Commander Yshan," she said.

Kyle grinned, feeling like a schoolboy. "Aw, shucks, Ma'am," he said. "I bet you say that to all the steely-eyed, heroic ship's captains who have just saved the Empire."

She chuckled. "All of them," she said and touched his hand.

"I think we deserve a holiday," Kyle said.

"I most enthusiastically agree," Charlotte replied.

Chapter 16

The wedding of Captain Kyle Yshan, Duke of the Moidari Sector, Guardian of the Six Home Planets and newly assigned to the Captaincy of the Battle Cruiser, *"Admiral Sestucal,"* flagship of the Yshan Galactic Fleet, to Charlotte Foster Bradshaw, only daughter of Joshua and Eleanor Bradshaw was truly a grand affair.

The ceremony took place in the Royal Palace on the Home World of Yshan and was attended by dignitaries from over two hundred planets within the Yshan Empire extending over two Galaxies, as well as the officers and men and women of the frigate, *"Charlie Foster,"* the previous command of Kyle Yshan. They were all in their "Ceremonial Whites," beautifully cut white tunics, black belts and officer-pattern swords with gold handles and their names engraved on the blades.

Also in attendance was His Imperial Majesty, Garamax the Nineteenth, Seventy-Second Emperor of the Yshan Galactic Empire. He sat in the front row with Charlotte's parents, dressed simply in a smart suit so as not to distract attention from the bridal couple.

Standing next to the groom as Best Man was Lieutenant-Commander Joshua Bradshaw, brother of the bride and grandson of the Fleet Commander, newly promoted and also assigned as Tactical Officer to the flagship Battle Cruiser in the Yshan Imperial Galactic Fleet.

When the ceremony had been completed by Fleet Admiral Joshua Bradshaw, Commander of the Twelve Sectors of the Galactic Fleet, the Best Man drew his sword and joined the other fleet personnel to form two lines holding their swords high, tips touching in the middle making a grand archway for the newly married couple to walk through.

The bride looked quite stunning and her parents both had tears running down their cheeks as she walked past them giving a beautiful smile in their direction.

The Empire's media made much of the fact that the last royal wedding had also been that of Charlotte to Kyle over a hundred and thirty years ago and the populations of the many planets throughout the Empire seemed delighted at this evidence of the restoration of old traditions.

The convoy of vehicles carrying the wedding party drove through the city streets, heavily lined with delighted observers and back to the Royal Palace for the private reception with the Emperor.

These proceedings were relaxed and informal but when Kyle saw a young officer enter the room and approach the Emperor, he sensed something critical had happened. The man spoke briefly to Henry then walked out. Henry saw Kyle observing the meeting and nodded at him, pointing briefly at Charlie and the Admiral, both of whom were engaged in cheerful conversations with others.

Kyle moved over to them and touched their shoulders and they followed him to join Henry.

"I just got the news," Henry said, some sadness in his face. "Both Sophie and Omaron died just minutes ago. The doctors say they collapsed and they resembled very, very old people at that moment."

"The last direct link with the Old Empire, barring yourself," said the Admiral.

"Indeed," said Henry with a nod. "Let's make sure this one stays peaceful until it's our turn to move on."

"Do you think that one day, we Yshans will be part of a new Star that we give to the next people to take over our world?" asked Charlie.

"Without a doubt," said Henry. "Now let's get back to the party. We have a new Empire to celebrate."

www.ingramcontent.com/pod-product-compliance
Lightning Source LLC
Chambersburg PA
CBHW072007170626
46813CB00005B/2053